EXT. RUST BELT AMERICA - DAWN

Haunting smokestacks and elevated highways.

INT. SCHOOL BUS - DAY

HUNTER is slouched in his seat, in sagged jeans and torn
shoes.

>HUNTER
>When is the skatepark opening?

>LYONS
>This summer, it'll be sick. No more
>skating only around the
>neighborhood—

>HUNTER
>No more harassing Plaza security
>guards?

>LYONS
>We can always fit that in!

Hunter spits on the floor.

>HUNTER
>I'm less enthused about this place.

>LYONS
>School?

>HUNTER
>I'm not going to graduate. It's a
>year of straight F's—

>LYONS
>Can you turn it around?

Hunter shrugs.

>HUNTER
>My wish is to find a girl.

>LYONS
>How will that change anything?

>HUNTER
>It will save me.

                    LYONS
          From who?

EXT. PUBLIC HIGH SCHOOL - DAY

Hunter and Lyons walk past a brutalist building lined with
flowers.

                    HUNTER
          I'm taking off after study hall. I
          can't be here today—

                    LYONS
          Where will you go?

                    HUNTER
          The Plaza. Let's meet up after you
          get out.

INT. CLASSROOM - DAY

A bell rings. Hunter's head is down on a desk, hood up on his
sweatshirt.

                    TEACHER
          Mister Yates. You have another slip
          for the principal's office.

Hunter rises and takes the slip.

                    TEACHER (CONT'D)
          Mister Freed, a doctor's
          appointment—

INT. HALLWAY - DAY

Hunter greets students in passing. The school runs like a
factory: a bell rings and halls clear.

INT. PRINCIPAL'S OFFICE - DAY

Hunter holds up the slip.

                    SECRETARY
          Go on, Principal Luther will see
          you now.

INT. PRINCIPAL'S ROOM - DAY

                    HUNTER
          Mister Luther.

                    LUTHER
          Good morning, Hunter. Let's see
          what you're here for today—
               (looks through papers)
          —skipping class. Do you ever plan
          to get your act together?

                    HUNTER
          I plan to make this a big year. I
          need to prepare for college—

                    LUTHER
          College? Mr. Yates, your
          disciplinary record is thicker than
          a dictionary. Which college do you
          plan to attend?

                    HUNTER
          I'm sure I can find one. I may pick
          up a sport to help my chances.

                    LUTHER
          A sport, Hunter? I'm going to give
          you two choices: you can take part
          in the Scared Straight program, and
          visit the regional prison. Or
          suspension for the rest of the
          year, effective immediately.

                    HUNTER
          But Principal Luther—

                    LUTHER
          You don't have a bright future at
          this school, and won't have a
          future at any college, either!

Hunter's eyes fill with tears.

                    LUTHER (CONT'D)
          Get your things together; your
          suspension begins now.

INT./EXT. POLICE CAR - DAY

Officer ZIMMERMAN drives through a derelict downtown. A phone
rings:

                    ZIMMERMAN
          Hi honey. How's the baby doing?

Whining emanates from his phone.

                    ZIMMERMAN (CONT'D)
          I'm sorry. Today's been a long one
          for me, too. Would you mind if I
          went with the guys—

More shrill noise.

                    ZIMMERMAN (CONT'D)
          I'll come home right after work. I
          love you.

EXT. BUS STOP - DAY

Hunter waits for a public bus, with a phone to his ear.

                    HUNTER
          What's up, Dirty?

                    DIRTY (O.S.)
              (raspy)
          We still skating?

                    HUNTER
          We'll have plenty of time; I got
          suspended again—

                    DIRTY (O.S.)
          'atta boy! I'll come over late
          afternoon—

The bus arrives and its doors open.

INT./EXT. POLICE CAR - DAY

Zimmerman's sirens flash, as a car pulls over in front of
him. He walks to the driver's window.

                    ZIMMERMAN
          License and registration.

He takes the documents and walks back to the police car.

EXT. DOWNTOWN - DAY

                    ZIMMERMAN
          Have you had anything to drink?

                    DRIVER
          No sir—

                    ZIMMERMAN
          What's the smell on your breath?

                    DRIVER
          Just had a bit, sir—

                    ZIMMERMAN
          Step out of the car.

The driver staggers as he gets out. In a flash of rage,
Zimmerman shoves him against the car.

                    ZIMMERMAN (CONT'D)
          Don't move. I'll be back with a
          breathalyzer.

Another police car pulls up.

                              DISSOLVE TO:

EXT. BEHIND THE PLAZA - DAY

Hunter practices flip tricks on a skateboard, as three boys
ride up and join.

                    LYONS
          What's up?

                    HUNTER
          Just kickin' around.

Lyons rolls past with WINSTON — who is tall and thin, with
crisp clothing — and J.R., who is small and scrappy.

                    J.R.
          This weekend looks like it's
          shaping up.

                    HUNTER
          Yeah?

                    J.R.
          Winston's parents are going away to
          visit his sister. We've been trying
          to line up beer and girls.

                    HUNTER
          Really?

> WINSTON
> Yeah, but I don't know if you can
> make it. We don't need any more
> dudes there.

Hunter is silent.

> WINSTON (CONT'D)
> I'm kidding. But you can't show up
> in that ragged hoodie.

J.R. snickers.

> LYONS
> Do you want to go to Ogden and
> skate, or stop by the railroad
> tracks first?

> WINSTON
> Let's head to the tracks.

INT. POLICE CAR - DAY

Zimmerman drives, as his police radio crackles.

> DISPATCHER (O.S.)
> Two-eighty, copy?

> ZIMMERMAN
> Two-eighty, go ahead.

> DISPATCHER (O.S.)
> We have a report of a missing
> vehicle, a doctor called it in.
> White Chevy Suburban, license plate
> GGP 1954.

> ZIMMERMAN
> Ten-four. Him again?

> DISPATCHER (O.S.)
> It was taken within the last hour.

> ZIMMERMAN
> I've picked up his kid for
> vandalism at the South Side Plaza—

He thinks for a moment:

> ZIMMERMAN (CONT'D)
> I bet he took the vehicle and drove
> over there.

Zimmerman pulls a U-turn and peels off.

EXT. RAILROAD TRACKS - DAY

Winston has a phone to his ear.

                    WINSTON
          That's excellent. We'll see you
          then!

He ends the call and turns to the other boys:

                    WINSTON (CONT'D)
          Marielle, Catalina, and her sister
          will get dropped off tomorrow
          night. They're bringing a case of
          beer.

                    HUNTER
          A case, for what, seven people?

                    WINSTON
          My parents have a few in our
          fridge, and there's the liquor
          cabinet—

                    HUNTER
          Dirty just texted me. He's on his
          way.

                    J.R.
          How do you know him again?

                    HUNTER
          He's the best skateboarder at my
          school. He was in Thrasher
          magazine: kickflipping the stairs
          downtown, the double set—

                    WINSTON
          Just make sure you don't tell him
          about tomorrow night. I don't trust
          this kid.

INT./EXT. POLICE CAR - DAY

Zimmerman patrols the Plaza. A few scattered stores are open,
but no one is around.

                    ZIMMERMAN
          Two-eighty, South Side Plaza. It's
          quiet down here.

                    DISPATCHER (O.S.)
              Two-eighty, stand by.

EXT. WOODS BY RAILROAD TRACKS - DAY

A figure pushes through foliage, down a path to the tracks.
He wears a dark nylon jacket and Brylcreemed black hair.

EXT. RAILROAD TRACKS - DAY

DIRTY steps out of the woods, and calls in a deep, raspy
voice:

                    DIRTY
              What up!

Hunter turns and exchanges a handshake; Winston and J.R. look
to each other. Dirty wears a backpack with a skateboard
tucked beneath.

                    HUNTER
              So, what about beer?

                    WINSTON
              We'll just have to make do.

                    DIRTY
              Why don't we snag some at the
              grocery store?

Winston is taken aback.

                    HUNTER
              We'll meet up with you guys later.

Dirty turns away, as Winston and Hunter make eye contact.

                    WINSTON
              Remember—

Hunter nods in confirmation.

EXT. PLAZA PATH - DUSK

Dirty and Hunter walk down a steep, wooded path from the
railroad tracks to the Plaza.

                    DIRTY
              I can't stand those kids.

                    HUNTER
          Winston?

                    DIRTY
          He's a conformist prick.

                    HUNTER
          He's been in private school all his
          life—

                    DIRTY
          Acting bossy, like he's some
          authority. I'd love to knock that
          kid out.

They drop their skateboards at the path's end.

EXT. BEHIND THE PLAZA - NIGHT

Hunter and Dirty walk through an alleyway, lit by sodium
lamps, to a small grocery store. They enter separately:
Hunter through a back entrance, Dirty through the front.

INT. GROCERY STORE - NIGHT

The store is old and understaffed. Dirty walks to the beer
aisle, holding his coat and backpack. Hunter approaches the
cash register.

                    HUNTER
          How are you?

                    EMPLOYEE
          Good. Good.

                    HUNTER
          My mother sent me for a pack of
          Virginia Slims.

                    EMPLOYEE
          Sure thing.

The employee walks to a service desk, where cigarettes are
kept behind glass. The MANAGER surveils the store.

INT. BEER AISLE - NIGHT

Dirty puts on his backpack backwards: on his chest.

INT. CASH REGISTER - CONTINUOUS

> MANAGER
> Do you have identification?

> HUNTER
> My mother sent me. She gave me a
> note to show you—

Hunter fumbles in his pockets.

> MANAGER
> Sorry, by law, we can't accept a
> note.

INT. BEER AISLE - CONTINUOUS

Dirty loads a twelve-pack of beer and loose bottles into the
backpack, still on his chest.

INT. CASH REGISTER - CONTINUOUS

> HUNTER
> I can't find the note. Are you sure
> you can't accept one? My mother
> will be furious—

> MANAGER
> I'm sorry.

INT. BEER AISLE - NIGHT

Dirty zips up his coat, over the backpack. He walks toward
the exit: with a bulbous, clanging belly.

INT. CASH REGISTER - NIGHT

> HUNTER
> I'll just get a Zero bar.

> MANAGER
> That's a better choice. Stay away
> from cigarettes, son.

INT. EXIT - NIGHT

Dirty walks out the front door, his back facing the cash
register.

INT. CASH REGISTER - NIGHT

Hunter pays for a candy bar and opens its wrapper.

                    HUNTER
          Thanks, guys.

They smile warmly. Hunter takes a bite and walks toward the
back door.

                    EMPLOYEE
          Have a good night—

EXT. PLAZA PATH - NIGHT

Dirty takes off the backpack and laughs fiendishly.

                    HUNTER
          The mother lode.

                    DIRTY
          I need to go back—

                    HUNTER
          Why?

                    DIRTY
          To get money for speedball.

                    HUNTER
          What do you have?

                    DIRTY
          Seven bucks. Leave the beer and
          stand at the edge of the path. If
          you see anyone coming, drop your
          skateboard to signal me.

EXT. BEHIND THE PLAZA - NIGHT

Dirty approaches a parked car and tests the door — it opens.

                                        CUT TO:

EXT. RAILROAD TRACKS - NIGHT

                    J.R.
          Do you want to bet on who can get
          Marielle?

He flashes a grin.

           WINSTON
Catalina is in calculus with me.
She might be valedictorian of our
class.

           J.R.
I'm surprised she's breaking from
homework to hang with our haggard
crew.

           WINSTON
I like Catalina a lot.

The rails beside them shimmer beneath the moon.

           J.R.
Why'd you invite Hunter?

           WINSTON
I wasn't going to. But he can get
us weed—

           LYONS
How about Catalina's sister? What's
her — *shit!*

Headlights catch them as a police car roars up. The boys take
off running, down the tracks and into the woods. Zimmerman
approaches with a flashlight. The rails begin thrumming;
light from an oncoming train appears in the distance.

           ZIMMERMAN
Come on out, boys!

He pauses, switching off the flashlight. He turns and walks
back, as a freight train thunders by.

EXT. PLAZA PATH - NIGHT

Dirty races up, looking shocked.

           HUNTER
Did you get money?

           DIRTY
We need to get out of here.

They turn and begin up the path.

           DIRTY (CONT'D)
I got something better. I'll show
you when we reach the tracks.

INT./EXT. POLICE CAR - NIGHT

Zimmerman drives in silence, as streetlights illuminate his face.

EXT. ALCOVE - NIGHT

Dirty and Hunter stop to catch their breaths, on a landing hidden by trees, far above the Plaza.

                    DIRTY
          Check this out.

He draws a handgun, moonlight glimmering across the metal.

                    HUNTER
          Damn—

Dirty pulls back the slide.

                    DIRTY
          It's loaded.

Hunter is frozen with fear. Dirty lets the slide snap back.

                    DIRTY (CONT'D)
          Who's the authority now?

                    HUNTER
          We need to hide it. If anybody saw
          you—

                    DIRTY
          Look how heavy it is.

                    HUNTER
          Plus your fingerprints. We need to
          ditch it—

                    DIRTY
          We'll ditch it near the tracks and
          come back tomorrow. They already
          might have called the cops.

They continue up the path, Hunter still stricken with fear.

                    DIRTY (CONT'D)
          I got money, too. Fuck the others.
          Let's call my boy and chill under
          the stars.

EXT. DOWNTOWN - MORNING

Imposing buildings and empty streets.

INT./EXT. POLICE CAR - DAY

Zimmerman wears sunglasses and sips a creamed coffee. His
phone rings:

                    ZIMMERMAN
          Is the baby feeling better today?

Monotonous complaining comes through.

                    ZIMMERMAN (CONT'D)
          I'm sorry—

More nagging.

                    ZIMMERMAN (CONT'D)
          We can make dinner if I'm not home
          too late—

An inaudible voice.

                    ZIMMERMAN (CONT'D)
          Of course that means I can make
          dinner.

He drives down a main street; no one is outside.

                    ZIMMERMAN (CONT'D)
          Hon, I've got a call coming in.
          I'll be home right after work—

EXT. RAILROAD TRACKS - DAY

Winston and J.R. walk along the tracks.

                    WINSTON
          There's your lighter—

                    J.R.
          I dropped my cigarettes, too.

                    WINSTON
          I don't see them—

                    J.R.
          Whatever, I have another pack.

                    WINSTON
          I talked with Catalina again. It
          seemed to go well, but sometimes I
          don't know what to say.

                    J.R.
          Just be assertive, or confident.
          That's what my brother says—

                    WINSTON
          Right. Let's go skate.

INT. POLICE STATION - DAY

Zimmerman pours a cup of coffee.

                    OFFICER
          We booked that drunk—

                    ZIMMERMAN
          This ain't the first time.

                    OFFICER
          It's the third—

                    ZIMMERMAN
          They just don't smarten up.

EXT. WOODS BY RAILROAD TRACKS - DAY

Hunter searches for the gun — it's gone.

                    HUNTER
               Fuck!

INT. POLICE STATION - DAY

                    OFFICER
          There's a report that a car was
          robbed, last night at the South
          Side Plaza.

                    ZIMMERMAN
          I chased some kids near there.
          They've been vandalizing buildings,
          but I don't know if they'd bust
          into a car—
               (sips coffee)
          What was reported missing?

                    OFFICER
          Loose bills and some change.

                    ZIMMERMAN
          When I run into those kids again,
          I'll confront them.

EXT. PLAZA FOUNTAIN - DAY

Hunter and Lyons meet at the Plaza's center.

                    HUNTER
          I'm done with school.

                    LYONS
          Done?

Hunter leaps onto an antiquated fountain.

                    HUNTER
          Suspended for the rest of the year.
          I don't want to go back—

                    LYONS
          What are you going to do?

                    HUNTER
          I don't know. Maybe find a way out
          of this place—

Hunter throws down his skateboard and kickflips off the
fountain.

                    LYONS
          Where will you go?

                    HUNTER
          New York City.

                    LYONS
          How can you afford it?

                    HUNTER
          I can't even afford the bus ticket.
          I don't know what to do—

Lyons looks at a text message.

                    LYONS
          Let's meet up with Winston and J.R.
          at Ogden.

INT. POLICE STATION - DAY

                    ZIMMERMAN
          Drunks, gangs, junkies—

                    OFFICER
          I ignore what I can.

                    ZIMMERMAN
          I just want to get my pension;
          maybe open a bar and retire to a
          cottage on a lake—

                    OFFICER
          I hear you. There aren't many
          stable jobs to support a family.

                    ZIMMERMAN
          That's all I'm here for, my family.

Zimmerman heads out on patrol.

                              DISSOLVE TO:

EXT. BEHIND AN ABANDONED FACTORY - DAY

Obstacles are set up for skateboarding — benches and parking
blocks — surrounded by rusted machinery and loading docks. A
dozen boys are skating.

                    J.R.
          Tonight's the night.

He clenches a cigarette between sewage-colored teeth.

                    HUNTER
          We snagged a twelver and some
          forties. I have them in a bag of
          ice—

                    J.R.
          What's this, the third time you
          crooks have stole beer?

                    HUNTER
          Yeah, plus candy, all the time.
          What's crazy is that Dirty broke
          into a car—

                    J.R.
          They should lock you guys up.

J.R. puffs from his cigarette, keeping a stern posture, as
Winston appears.

                    WINSTON
          Excited for girls tonight?

                    HUNTER
          Hell yeah.

                    WINSTON
          Everyone at my school has been
          partying with girls this year;
          finally our time has come.

                    HUNTER
          Hopefully we can get them drunk!

                    WINSTON
          This girl Catalina and her sister
          Rachel are perfect. I really want
          Catalina, always staring at her in
          class—

A police car creeps around the side of the factory, a few
yards from where the boys are skating.

INT./EXT. POLICE CAR - DAY

The driver's window is down:

                    ZIMMERMAN
          Don't move!

The boys brace themselves, uncertain about what to do.
Suddenly, they take off running — except for Hunter and
Lyons.

EXT. WOODS BY RAILROAD TRACKS - DAY

Winston sprints, weaving through trees, as J.R. and younger
boys trail behind. They stop at the tracks, out of breath.

                    WINSTON
          I can't wait until we're in college
          and can put this shit behind us—

EXT. BEHIND AN ABANDONED FACTORY - DAY

Zimmerman approaches Hunter and Lyons.

                    ZIMMERMAN
          You little shits broke into a car
          at the South Side Plaza?

Hunter's eyes open wide.

                    ZIMMERMAN (CONT'D)
          What did you take?

EXT. WOODS BY RAILROAD TRACKS - DAY

                    J.R.
          I think Hunter wants to be a kid
          forever. Him and that dope fiend he
          hangs out with—

                    WINSTON
               (sneering)
          Losers.

EXT. BEHIND AN ABANDONED FACTORY - DAY

                    HUNTER
          We didn't do anything—

Lyons steps back.

                    ZIMMERMAN
          Tell the truth!

Zimmerman clenches Hunter's collar.

                    ZIMMERMAN (CONT'D)
          The truth!

Lyons runs away.

                    HUNTER
          Get off, pig!

EXT. WOODS BY RAILROAD TRACKS - DAY

Lyons races through the woods.

EXT. BEHIND AN ABANDONED FACTORY - DAY

Zimmerman is power-mad, gripping Hunter's collar.

                    ZIMMERMAN
          This city is bad enough; I'm not
          letting you make it worse!

                    HUNTER
          Get off!

EXT. WOODS BY RAILROAD TRACKS - DAY

Lyons reaches the others, shocked.

                    LYONS
          That goon was getting rough with
          us.

                    WINSTON
          Did he get Hunter?

                    LYONS
          Yeah—

                    J.R.
            (scoffs)
          Let's go home and shower; the girls
          will be here soon.

EXT. BEHIND AN ABANDONED FACTORY - DAY

Zimmerman grips him tighter.

                    HUNTER
          Get off! Or I'll put a fucking
          trademark across—

Zimmerman savagely backhands him across the mouth.

                    ZIMMERMAN
          Get the fuck out of here.

Hunter's eyes well up, as he takes off running.

                                        DISSOLVE TO:

INT. LIVING ROOM - NIGHT

Winston, J.R., and Lyons sip liquor. The doorbell rings.

                    WINSTON
          Let the festivities begin.

INT. DOORWAY - NIGHT

                    MARIELLE
          Hey!

                    RACHEL
          Hey, guys—

The girls enter Winston's large, comfortable home.

                    WINSTON
          Here, let us put those in the
          fridge—

J.R. takes a case of beer and walks into the kitchen.

INT. LIVING ROOM - NIGHT

                    WINSTON
          Can I interest you in a rum and
          Coke?

                    MARIELLE
          Sure—

                    CATALINA
          Where are your parents?

                    WINSTON
          They went to Brown University to
          visit my sister.

                    CATALINA
          That's impressive. I applied to
          Brown.

                    WINSTON
          Hopefully we'll get our acceptance
          letters soon.

                    CATALINA
          Or rejection letters. I'm nervous—

                    WINSTON
          What's your first choice?

                    CATALINA
          I'm hoping for Cornell. But I also
          applied to Penn and some safeties.

                    WINSTON
          I can't wait to get past high
          school: have an adult life, pledge
          for a fraternity—

                    CATALINA
          Yeah.

INT./EXT. POLICE CAR - NIGHT

Zimmerman patrols downtown streets, passing by boarded-up
storefronts.

                    DISPATCHER (O.S.)
          We have a report of suspicious
          activity at the warehouses between
          North Street and Johnson Avenue.

                    ZIMMERMAN
          Ten-four. I'll check it out.

INT. LIVING ROOM - NIGHT

                    MARIELLE
          All we have is a case and half a
          rum bottle?

                    WINSTON
          A guy we know has more, and is
          supposed to swing by. But we don't
          know what happened—

                    J.R.
          He got picked up by the cops.

                    CATALINA
          Who is he?

                    WINSTON
          Just some kid from around the
          neighborhood.

                    J.R.
          He said something about breaking
          into a car, too—

                    WINSTON
          Just some deviant kid.

INT./EXT. POLICE CAR - NIGHT

Zimmerman creeps with a spotlight. Ghostly factories loom in
the distance, with rows of broken windows.

INT. LIVING ROOM - NIGHT

The doorbell rings.

                    WINSTON
          That may be our beer.

INT. DOORWAY - NIGHT

Hunter stands with a swollen lip and backpack.

                    WINSTON
          That lip is looking gorgeous.

                    HUNTER
          That coward Lyons ran away. I went
          at it with that cop alone.

                    WINSTON
          Did you bring beer?

                    HUNTER
          Yeah, in my bag.

INT. LIVING ROOM - NIGHT

                    WINSTON
          This is Hunter.

                    HUNTER
          Nice to meet you—

                    WINSTON
          Here, let me put those in the
          fridge.

Hunter opens the backpack.

                    RACHEL
          What happened to your lip?

                    HUNTER
          I had a scuffle—

                    J.R.
          He's a misfit.

                    CATALINA
               (smirks)
          He's a bad boy?

INT./EXT. POLICE CAR - NIGHT

Zimmerman's light meanders along graffiti-covered walls. His
phone rings:

                    ZIMMERMAN
          Hello?

                    BURNS (O.S.)
          Officer Zimmerman? This is
          Detective Burns.

                    ZIMMERMAN
          How are you?

                    BURNS (O.S.)
          Good, thanks. I see that you've
          submitted several reports from the
          South Side Plaza. What's the deal
          over there?

                    ZIMMERMAN
          The usual, dilapidated place.
          Vandalism, stealing—

INT. LIVING ROOM - NIGHT

Hunter sits on the floor and sketches on scrap paper.

                    CATALINA
          What are you drawing?

                    HUNTER
          Just a cartoon.

                    CATALINA
          That's cute.

Winston glances at them from across the room.

                    WINSTON
          Catalina, may I get you another
          beer?

                    CATALINA
          Sure.

He walks over.

                    WINSTON
          Have you thought about college
          majors yet?

                    CATALINA
          Maybe government or public policy—

He hands her a bottle.

                    WINSTON
          I love that shirt, by the way.

INT./EXT. POLICE CAR - NIGHT

                    ZIMMERMAN
          I'm headed to the South Side Plaza—

                    BURNS (O.S.)
          There was a car robbed the other
          day. What do you know about it?

                    ZIMMERMAN
          Only that it happened.

                    BURNS (O.S.)
          We've opened an investigation—

                    ZIMMERMAN
          Over spare change?

INT. LIVING ROOM - NIGHT

Winston glares at Hunter and Catalina laughing together.

                    WINSTON
          Does everybody want to go to the
          church and skate?

                    LYONS
          Drunk, at this hour?

                    MARIELLE
          Where's the church?

                    WINSTON
          It's down the street. Let's go.

INT. POLICE CAR - NIGHT

                    BURNS (O.S.)
          We got the report that the car was
          robbed. Then we received a follow
          up.

                    ZIMMERMAN
          And?

                    BURNS (O.S.)
          The guy who owns it had a forty-
          five caliber handgun in the
          glovebox. It wasn't locked, and the
          gun is missing.

                    ZIMMERMAN
          Jesus.

EXT. STREET - NIGHT

Hunter and Catalina walk together, trailing the others.

                    CATALINA
          It's a beautiful view of the valley
          from here.

                    HUNTER
          That's the South Side Plaza down
          there, and the river beyond it.

                    CATALINA
          Those lights from the houses are
          pretty—

                    HUNTER
          You should see from the church
          roof. We can climb up there.

                    CATALINA
          That sounds lovely.

EXT. STREET - NIGHT

Winston appears, standing erect.

                    WINSTON
          We need to stay quiet; the
          neighbors will call the cops if
          they hear us.

                    CATALINA
               (softly)
          It's a gorgeous neighborhood—

                    WINSTON
          You'll have to come around more
          often.

He touches the back of her arm.

INT. POLICE CAR - NIGHT

                    BURNS (O.S.)
          We've had several reports about a
          doctor's kid, and the doctor
          contacted us—

                    ZIMMERMAN
          I know the kid you're talking
          about; they call him Dirty. There's
          a group of them—

                                        CUT TO:

EXT. CHURCH - NIGHT

                    WINSTON
          Do you want to see who can kickflip
          the stairs first?

                    HUNTER
          Sure, let's go.

EXT. CHURCH - CONTINUOUS

Winston skates up and hurls himself down the stairs. The
board zips out from beneath him.

                    J.R.
               Come on!

EXT. CHURCH - CONTINUOUS

Hunter approaches, as streetlights illuminate his face. He
snaps the board into the air — spinning the trick beneath him
— before losing control of it.

                    RACHEL
          Careful!

EXT. CHURCH - CONTINUOUS

Hunter is short of breath. Winston looks at him
contemptuously.

>   WINSTON
>   Determination is a masculine
>   quality.

EXT. CHURCH - NIGHT

Winston attempts the trick; his board zips out again. Hunter
barrels up, spins the kickflip, and lands it cleanly. He
looks toward Winston:

>   HUNTER
>   And so is winning.

INT. POLICE CAR - NIGHT

>   BURNS (O.S.)
>   The guy who owns the car knew about
>   the money, but didn't notice the
>   missing gun until this afternoon.

>   ZIMMERMAN
>   You're sure they might not have
>   been taken separately?

>   BURNS (O.S.)
>   With rampant theft at the South
>   Side Plaza, and normally the guy
>   keeps the car in his garage—

>   ZIMMERMAN
>   What's he doing with a gun in his
>   glovebox?

>   BURNS (O.S.)
>   God knows.

EXT. CHURCH - NIGHT

>   J.R.
>   Let's see who can lipslide the
>   ledge first—

>   WINSTON
>   I'm game.

                    MARIELLE
          What's a lipslide?

                    J.R.
          Here, I'll show you.

                    HUNTER
          I'm going to grab another beer—

Hunter picks up his backpack and looks to Catalina:

                    HUNTER (CONT'D)
          Want to go up there?

EXT. ROOFTOP - NIGHT

Hunter and Catalina lift themselves onto the church roof, a
vista far above the valley. She inhales deeply.

                    CATALINA
          —delicious, what is that?

                    HUNTER
          It's bread baking. There's a
          factory in the valley that makes
          it, late at night.

                    CATALINA
          That's amazing—

Hunter opens a malt liquor bottle and takes a swig.

                    HUNTER
          The valley might look nice from up
          here, but on the ground it's rough.

                    CATALINA
          I bet you're anxious to leave in
          the fall—

                    HUNTER
          I wish that I didn't have to be.

                    CATALINA
          It's a big world, lots to explore—

                    HUNTER
          But this is home.

She takes in the night air. He takes her hand; they slowly
kiss.

INT. KITCHEN - MORNING

Sunlight pours through open blinds.

INT. HALLWAY - DAY

Zimmerman walks down a staircase. He puts on his duty belt
and secures the handgun.

INT. ROOM - DAY

Zimmerman slips into a side room, where a baby sleeps in a
crib. He bends down and kisses its forehead.

                    ZIMMERMAN
          Sleep tight, sweet prince.

EXT. PUBLIC HIGH SCHOOL - DAY

Hunter enters an empty basketball court. Dirty approaches
from the opposite side, wearing a hooded sweatshirt with an
American flag printed on it.

                    HUNTER
          Do you have it?

                    DIRTY
          Yeah, I picked it up early
          yesterday. I fired it, too.

                    HUNTER
          Where?

                    DIRTY
          In a field near my house. It felt
          incredible — a release of anger,
          frustration, everything.

Dirty lights a cigarette.

                    HUNTER
          Where'd you get those?

                    DIRTY
          I found them at the railroad
          tracks.

                    HUNTER
          J.R. smokes that brand—

Dirty picks up his skateboard.

                    DIRTY
          Have you tried the handrail?

                    HUNTER
          No, you?

                    DIRTY
          Yeah, but never landed it.

Dirty throws down the board and barrels toward a handrail. He
snaps into the air and slides down, before bailing out.

                    HUNTER
          Do you ever feel that skating is
          all we have?

                    DIRTY
          Hell yeah, maybe someday it will
          take us out of here.

                    HUNTER
          Save us from school, the fucking
          cops, everything—

Dirty smirks. Hunter jumps on his board and attempts the
handrail. The board slips and he falls hard.

                    DIRTY
          It isn't school or the cops that
          keep you down!

                    HUNTER
          Who is it, then?

                    DIRTY
          It's your friends. We need to be
          saved from our friends.

Dirty tries the rail again, coming close to landing it.

                    HUNTER
          What about a girl?

                    DIRTY
          What about one?

                    HUNTER
          I need one—

                    DIRTY
          You need to focus on you: save
          yourself and the rest will come.

Hunter throws down his board and slides the rail, landing it
perfectly.

                    DIRTY (CONT'D)
          Damn!

EXT. PUBLIC HIGH SCHOOL - DAY

Hunter walks back to him and speaks softly:

                    HUNTER
          So, what do you want to do?

                    DIRTY
          With the gun?

                    HUNTER
          Yeah.

                    DIRTY
          The guy that I get junk from wants
          to trade. But I'm worried about
          keeping it at my house any longer—

                    HUNTER
          Give it to me, and I'll keep it
          safe.

Dirty grabs his backpack, draws the gun, smiles, and passes
it to Hunter.

                    DIRTY
          Take care of my nickel-plated baby.

INT./EXT. POLICE CAR - DAY

Zimmerman is on the phone, driving.

                    ZIMMERMAN
          The doctor's kid stole his old
          man's vehicle again. His wife just
          called it in—

                    BURNS (O.S.)
          We've been in contact; they heard a
          round fired yesterday. His kid has
          the gun—

                    ZIMMERMAN
          What should I do?

                    BURNS (O.S.)
          Isolate the other kids. We'll take
          down Mister Dirty the cleanest way
          we can.

EXT. RAILROAD TRACKS - DAY

Hunter approaches Lyons, showdown-style.

                    HUNTER
          What's up?

                    LYONS
          Listen, I'm sorry—

                    HUNTER
          It's cool.

                    LYONS
          What did he do to you?

                    HUNTER
          He backhanded me. But it's cool.
          Check this out—

Hunter draws the gun.

                    LYONS
          —*shit.*

Lyons is intimidated, afraid.

                    HUNTER
          Dirty lifted it from a car.

                    LYONS
          What are you going to do with it?

                    HUNTER
          I need to get rid of it, before
          Dirty creates a nightmare.

                    LYONS
          We're headed to the island tonight
          for a bonfire and beers. Meet us—

                    HUNTER
          I'll throw the gun in the river
          when I cross the dam. But I need to
          see Catalina first.

                    LYONS
          What happened with her?

                    HUNTER
          She's the one for me. But I don't
          know what to do—

                    LYONS
          Why don't you catch a public bus to
          her house?

                    HUNTER
          —are you sure?

                    LYONS
          Sometimes you have to take a
          chance.

INT./EXT. POLICE CAR - DAY

Zimmerman drives in silence.

                                        MATCH CUT TO:

INT./EXT. PUBLIC BUS - DAY

Hunter gazes out a window.

EXT. FRONT PORCH - DAY

Hunter rings Catalina's doorbell and waits for an answer.

                    CATALINA
          Hey!

                    HUNTER
          How are you?

Catalina holds up a thick envelope with a red design that
reads Cornell University.

                    CATALINA
          I got in!

                    HUNTER
          That's fantastic—

                    CATALINA
          It's such a relief, after all the
          worrying. Come inside—

INT. KITCHEN - DAY

Catalina's house is old and disheveled. There is a pineapple on the table.

                    CATALINA
          I was just about to cut this — my
          favorite.

                    HUNTER
          That looks delicious. Are your
          parents excited by your acceptance?

                    CATALINA
          They are, but it will bring new
          pressures. It's going to be
          expensive—

She slices into the pineapple.

                    HUNTER
          Won't you be able to take a loan?

                    CATALINA
          I will, but the whole thing is
          costly. My mom's hours got cut back
          at work.

                    HUNTER
          Don't they say the hardest part is
          getting in? I have faith that you
          can make it work.

She smiles.

                    CATALINA
          I'll need to find a job during
          college, which is stressful. But I
          agree, if I've made it this far—

                    HUNTER
          I can't see you being anything but
          successful, and can't imagine the
          opportunities that will open up.

They lean in and kiss.

                    CATALINA
          Care for some pineapple?

He takes a piece.

                    HUNTER
          I'm not so confident about my
          prospects.

                    CATALINA
          Why not?

                    HUNTER
          My school situation is a disaster.
          I'm always dragged down by other
          people.

                    CATALINA
          Maybe you need to get away from all
          that, and go to a college near me?

She smiles and takes a slice of pineapple.

                    HUNTER
          Does that mean we can still see
          each other when you're climbing the
          ladder to success?

                    CATALINA
          Of course we can. I mean, if that's
          what you want—

                    HUNTER
          I don't want to lose you when the
          summer ends.

                    CATALINA
          Aw, you won't. I'll always be here—

                    HUNTER
          I suppose you'll have winter break
          free?

                    CATALINA
          Of course. But what's important is
          getting you on the ladder of
          success with me.

She squeezes his hand.

                    HUNTER
          Things are changing; I'm
          optimistic.

They kiss again.

                                        DISSOLVE TO:

EXT. BEHIND THE PLAZA - DUSK

Hunter singes his lips on a roach clip, as he observes a
police car from the hill above. He turns and walks down a
secluded path.

EXT. PLAZA PATH - DUSK

Hunter looks beyond the highway below, to a flickering light
in the middle of the river.

EXT. HIGHWAY - DUSK

Hunter runs to a canopied parking lot. Storm clouds fill the
sky. Fire rises on the island, visible through foliage,
across a narrow dam.

EXT. PARKING LOT - CONTINUOUS

Hunter crosses the parking lot toward a wooded path, leading
down to the dam. Raindrops pelt the metal canopy. He looks
back — a police car roars into the parking lot.

EXT. WOODED PATH - CONTINUOUS

Hunter races toward the river. The dam and fire are ahead,
enveloped by a black river and bruised sky. He looks back—

EXT. WOODED PATH - CONTINUOUS

Zimmerman grabs Hunter's collar and pulls him down.

                    HUNTER
          Let go!

                    ZIMMERMAN
          What are you running from!

                    HUNTER
          Let me go!

Zimmerman backhands him across the face, sending Hunter down
into mud and rocks, with blood on his lips.

                    ZIMMERMAN
          Get up, boy!

Hunter draws the gun from his pants, with fire in his eyes.
He pulls the trigger.

INT. BEDROOM - MORNING

Television news drones on.

INT. BEDROOM - DAY

> NEWS ANCHOR (O.S.)
> A police officer was slain
> yesterday in a riverside chase. The
> perpetrator is in custody.

Principal Luther's face appears on screen:

> LUTHER
> —suspended from school; his own
> worst enemy. This animal couldn't
> save himself—

INT. BEDROOM - DAY

Catalina stares at the television.

> CATALINA
> I'm not going to let this knock me
> off track—

Tears run down her cheeks.

> CATALINA (CONT'D)
> I'm not going to let this...my
> bright future...

INT./EXT. SCHOOL BUS - DAY

Lyons sits alone, reading from a tablet; a stunned look hits
his face.

> LYONS
> Fuck.

CUT TO BLACK